CORRINNE
AVERISS

KIRSTI
BEAUTYMAN

love

words & pictures

Everyone loved everyone in Tess's house.

Daddy loved Mummy, Mummy loved Daddy.
Tess loved Mummy and Daddy and Tom.
Everyone loved Tom, and Tom loved everyone else...

...apart from Diggle,
who barked loudly and
scared him sometimes.

But Diggle loved everyone too.

Mum said, "Loving someone means
you like being near them.
As near as you can possibly get!"

For Wren, our little outside
heart on a string. – C.A.

For Ryan. Our love will always
stretch to reach. – K.B.

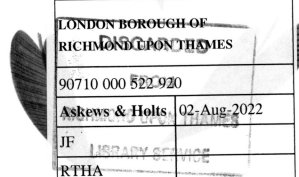

Brimming with creative inspiration, how-to
projects, and useful information to enrich your
everyday life, quarto.com is a favorite destination
for those pursuing their interests and passions.

Inspiring | Educating | Creating | Entertaining

© 2020 Quarto Publishing plc
Text © 2020 Corrinne Averiss
Illustrations © 2020 Kirsti Beautyman

Corrinne Averiss has asserted her right to be identified as the author of this work.
Kirsti Beautyman has asserted her right to be identified as the illustrator of this work.

First published in paperback
in 2022 by words & pictures,
an imprint of The Quarto Group.
The Old Brewery, 6 Blundell Street,
London N7 9BH, United Kingdom.
T (0)20 7700 6700 F (0)20 7700 8066
www.quarto.com

A catalogue record for this book is available from the British Library.

ISBN: 978 0 7112 7261 3
eISBN: 978 0 7112 5548 7

Manufactured in Guangdong, China TT082022

9 8 7 6 5 4 3 2 1

MIX
Paper from
responsible sources
FSC® C016973
FSC
www.fsc.org

Tess thought about all the love that filled their home, like the light inside one of Daddy's little houses.

If Tess had to leave home, then
Mummy or Daddy went with her.

And so the love came too
– wherever she went – and
kept her warm, like a scarf.

When Tess visited Granny and Gramps's
house, the love she had left there last time
was still safe inside.

Tess always had love nearby.

But one sunny September day,
it was time for Tess to start school.

Mummy and Daddy couldn't come to school.
Tom was too little, Granny and Gramps were too big...

...and dogs can't use crayons.

So Tess would have to be brave all by herself.

School was large, with lots of doors and windows.
It wasn't like a candle house or a warm scarf.

"If we're not together, will the love still find me?" asked Tess.

"Don't worry," said Mum. "Love is like a string between us – it can stretch as far as it needs to."

They said goodbye at the gate.

It felt strange to Tess, not having love near.

How could she know that Mummy was on the end of her string?

She tugged, but perhaps Mummy was already too far away to feel it.

Tess ran right up to the school gate.
She might be closer that way.

She tugged again.

"Are you okay, Tess?" A teacher had joined her.

"I don't know if Mummy is on the end of my string," Tess explained.
The teacher gave Tess a cuddle. She was called Mrs Turley, and
she understood.

"I promise, your Mummy is
always on the end!" she said.

As they walked back to the classroom,
Tess noticed a little thread between them.

That felt nice.

Mrs Turley guided Tess to a table, where
a boy was making a paper dragon.
"Do you want to help?" he asked,
and offered her the glue.

As they played, Tess told the boy all about her strings.
"I have strings too!" said the boy, excitedly.

He was called Harry and one of his strings was very special. It stretched far away because his daddy had died when he was small.
"It goes up, up high", Harry explained.

Now Tess had a string with her new friend, too.

The more she looked, the more
Tess saw that everyone had strings.

Love that went
sideways, backwards,
forwards and upwards.

At home time, she felt a little tug
on her string as she thought about
Mummy waiting for her at the gate.

Tess stood with Mrs Turley and watched, as one by one, all the children were met with a cuddle and left for home.

Where was her Mummy?
Tess's tummy fluttered
and her heart beat fast.
Her sadness turned to worry.
And she tugged the string again
and again to see if anyone was there.

Mrs Turley took her back into the classroom to wait. It seemed to Tess that her string was useless.

IT WASN'T CONNECTING HER TO ANYTHING!

With trembling hands, she untied
the knot and let it fall to the floor.

Then Tess cried and cried, and
though Mrs Turley tried to help,
she wanted to be alone.

Suddenly she felt a hand
on her shoulder... Mummy!

"I'm so sorry Tess. Tom was
crying for his lost teddy.
It took us ages to find it!"
Tess hugged Mummy tightly.

Then she remembered
what she had done.
"I untied our string!"
Tess confessed, sadly.

"Well, let's fix that," said Mummy, smiling. She looped the string, pulled the knot and reconnected them.

Everything felt right again.
"I promise you Tess, our string may stretch or
tangle, but it will never truly break," said Mummy.

Then Mummy and Tess cried happy tears,
and felt their love wrap them in a big bundle...

...and roll them all the way home.